PONY CAMP diaries

Emily and Emerald

For Austen with thanks xx

tiger tales

5 River Road, Suite 128, Wilton, CT 06897
Published in the United States 2019
Originally published in Great Britain in 2007
by the Little Tiger Group

ISBN-13: 978-1-68010-165-2
ISBN-10: 1-68010-165-X
Printed in China
STP/1800/0254/0219

10 9 8 7 6 5 4 3 2 1

For more insight and activities, visit us at www.tigertalesbooks.com

PONY CAMP diaries

Emily and Emerald

by Kelly McKain

Illustrated by Mandy Stanley

tiger tales

Other titles in the series:

Megan and Mischief

Penny and Prince

Chloe and Cookie

Sophie and Sparkle

Cassie and Charm

THIS DIARY BELONGS TO

Contents

Dear Riders,

A warm welcome to Sunnyside Stables!

Sunnyside is our home, and for the next week it will be yours, too! We're a big family—my husband, Jason, and I have two children, Olivia and Tyler, plus two dogs ... and all the ponies, of course!

We have friendly yard staff and a very talented instructor, Sally, to help you get the most out of your week. If you have any worries or questions about anything at all, just ask. We're here to help, and we want your vacation to be as enjoyable as possible—so don't be shy!

As you know, you will have a pony to take care of as your own for the week. Your pony can't wait to meet you and start having fun! During your stay, you'll be caring for your pony, improving your riding, enjoying long rides in the country, learning new skills, and making new friends. Add swimming, games, movies, barbecues, and a gymkhana, and you're in for a fun-filled vacation to remember!

This special Pony Camp Diary is for you to fill with your vacation memories. We hope you'll write all about your adventures here at Sunnyside Stables—because we know you're going to have a lot of them!

Wishing you a wonderful time with us!

Jess xx

manège
stables x 4
farmhouse & yard
stables x 2
yard
pool
Tack room
parking lot
office
Cooper
lower field

Sunnyside Stables

hay barn

stables x 4

feed room

stables x 4

Barn

here I am on

EMERALD

To upper fields →

Monday—I can't believe I'm really here at Pony Camp!

I feel EXCITED about being here, but NERVOUS at the same time!

I'm EXCITED 'cos I haven't ridden since we moved here from Philadelphia three weeks ago —I can't wait to get back in the saddle! And I'm NERVOUS because at the stables where I used to ride and help out on weekends, there were these older girls and … well, I don't really want to write all about what happened with them in my beautiful new Pony Camp Diary. And, anyway, this is meant to be a new beginning.

Actually, me and Mom are both getting a fresh start down here in Milton. Since it's summer vacation, I haven't started at my new school yet, so it's been a bit boring 'cos I've just been helping Mom unpack boxes and paint the living room.

I felt extra NERVOUS when Jess showed us up here to my room. I wanted Mom to stay for a while, but she had to go back to the new house and wait for the electrician, so I ended up on my own. There are three beds in here, and Jess said the one by the window was her daughter Olivia's, so I had the choice out of the bunk beds. I went for the bottom one, and as I started unpacking my stuff, I could hear all this noise and laughter coming from the room next door.

The two girls in there were really loud and confident—the exact opposite of ME! Then I heard all these footsteps on the stairs and someone yelling, "Hey, Charlie!" at the top of their voice. For one second I thought there was a BOY at Pony Camp, but then I heard this girl's voice yelling back, and I realized that Charlie must be short for Charlotte.

And that was when Frankie bustled in with her mom, who is also really loud and who kept on calling her Francesca. I felt really shy and I wished I could shrink into a corner and disappear. But when Frankie rolled her eyes at me, I couldn't help smiling. She shooed her mom out and said hello, and after a few seconds of me blushing shyly with no words coming out, I finally managed to mumble, "Hi, I'm Emily."

Frankie said, "Hi, Ems. Call me Frankie—everyone does. Well, except for her, of course!"

She waved toward the door, obviously meaning her mom. "And my big sister Charlie when she's trying to annoy me! That's her loud voice you can hear, by the way—she has such a big mouth!"

I smiled as she threw her stuff on the top bunk. No one's ever called me Ems before—I really like it. I was trying to think of something to say when Charlie put her head around the door and shouted, "Come on, Frog Face, we're all going down to the yard!"

She grabbed Frankie's arm and started pulling her out of the room. Frankie giggled and cried, "Don't call me Frog Face, Monkey Breath!" Then Frankie tried to grab my arm, and I wanted to go with them, but my feet stayed stuck to the spot. For some reason, I don't seem to be that good at joining in.

"I'll be down in a sec!" I told them as brightly as I could. "I just want to start off my diary first."

So that's what I've been doing!

Oh, hang on, even the other room with the younger girls in it is quiet, so everyone must be outside. Okay, I'm going to take a deep breath and put on my hat and body protector (and a big smile) and go down to the yard.

Monday 1:45 p.m.—well, I still can't believe what happened this morning!

I'm so EXCITED and NERVOUS again! EXCITED because I have met the most amazing pony named Emerald, who I'm desperate to have as my own for the week. And NERVOUS because I'm waiting to hear from Sally, our instructor, about whether I can have her or not.

Sally went to speak to Jason about it (he's the yard manager and also Olivia's dad), and she said she'll come and find me after lunch. We've finished eating now, and I'm writing this sitting at the picnic table outside the farmhouse so I can keep a lookout for her.

Okay, well, this is a pic of (fingers crossed!) my fabulous pony, Emerald!

She isn't supposed to be one of the Pony Camp ponies at all, but as soon as I saw her

I knew I wanted her, and Sally did admit it seems like Emerald has chosen me, too. But she also said I'd have to ride Flame first in the assessment and, whoops, I'm trying to say everything at once and messing things up. Okay, I'll take a deep breath and slow down and write everything in order.

So I headed over to the yard to find the others, and as I walked between the parking lot and lower field, this pony came bolting toward me, completely loose, with a head collar on and her lead rope dangling. It was Emerald!

I didn't know her name then, of course. And I didn't know that she'd just arrived at Sunnyside and had bolted out of the trailer as Sally was unloading her. But I did know that she was the most beautiful pony I'd ever seen.

She was skittering around, looking really scared. For a moment I froze in shock, but then I thought how dangerous that dangling lead rope was, and how I had to stop her from tripping on it and having an accident.

I stood my ground as she came right up to me, and I spread my arms out so that she couldn't get past and gallop off up the track to the upper fields.

I took a deep breath and tried to relax. Emerald lowered her head and snorted; she seemed to be calming down a bit, too. I stepped toward her and put my hand out for her to smell.

"Be careful!" Sally called as she appeared around the corner. I gave a slight nod, then slowly turned so I was standing at Emerald's shoulder and reached down for the end of the lead rope. Then I stood there with both hands on the rope while Sally came over and took it from me. "Great job!" she said softly. "You showed a lot of horse sense by staying so calm."

I smiled, and inside I was really proud of myself.

Sally asked my name, and just when I thought she was going to send me off to the yard to join the others, she said I could help take Emerald into the barn instead. She told me to lead her into a small pen in the corner, away from the other ponies. As I walked her, I kept glancing at her shiny, glossy bay coat and cute white star and big brown eyes and thinking how beautiful and special she was.

We got some hay for her and filled up her water trough, and as I was rubbing her nose to say good-bye, I blurted out to Sally, "Do you think maybe I could have Emerald as my pony this week?"

Sally frowned. "I'm sorry, Emily, but she's not going to be ridden at Pony Camp for a while," she said. "She's very nervous, and I need to work with her myself first."

I tried to smile, but I couldn't hide how disappointed I was. Emerald leaned her head over the railing and nudged my arm. I rubbed her neck, and she snorted gently.

"It wouldn't be an easy week," Sally said then. I stared at her. Was she saying yes after all? "I've ridden Emerald myself, and I know her temperament and capabilities," she continued. "You won't be able to do any jumping with her, and you'll have to keep her calm in flat work or she might charge off with you."

"I don't mind," I insisted. "I don't care about any of that; I just want to be with Emerald."

Sally smiled. "I know you do, Emily, but we have to be sensible. I'll need you to ride another pony in the assessment lesson, so I can see what level you're at. And then we'll think about it. Okay?"

"Okay!" I cried, grinning.

So I gave Emerald one last pat and showed her that I had my fingers crossed for us. Then Sally and I went to join the others, who were all hanging around outside the office, squished on to the bench and chatting away. I hung back behind Sally as we neared them. I wish I could just talk to new people like that, as if I've known them forever. Frankie and the others make it look so easy.

Everyone had already introduced themselves, but Sally got them to say their names to me, too, which made me the center of attention and left me feeling completely embarrassed!

The other girls are:

Charlotte said she and Chantelle and Elena (she's Spanish so you say it Elay-na) are all 12 and in the same class at school. They're sharing a room in the farmhouse, too. Madison and Morgan are 8 and 9, and they've come all the way from New York. They're staying with their grandma for the summer, and she had the idea of sending them to Pony Camp. They're sharing the other room with Neema, who just turned 9. Me and Frankie are both 10, almost 11, and we're sharing a room with Olivia.

The girls all seemed really nice, and as Sally read the Safety in the Yard rules, I wished I could just pile onto the bench, too, but I stayed put. I didn't dare join in with everyone, in case one of them shoved me off. Maybe that sounds like a strange thing to say, but the older girls at my last yard seemed nice at first, too, and they turned out to be really horrible, so I can't help thinking that kind of stuff.

Luckily, everyone had to get up then 'cos we were going on a tour around Sunnyside. We found out about the fire drill meeting points, and we were learning the safety stuff as we went around—like in the tack room Sally told us that we must put any brushes or numnahs and things away after using them, and in the yard she showed us how to tie up a pony safely.

As we walked around, everyone was chattering together in a big group, so I just smiled and tried to join in here and there. When Sally showed us the barn, everyone went completely crazy over the ponies that were being tacked up for us. But I was just gazing at Emerald, who was standing in her little pen, looking back at me.

Then it was time to get matched up with our ponies. Back in the yard, everyone started to pull on their hats and gloves, chatting excitedly. Sally got her list and read off who was on who, as Jess and Lydia, the stable girl, led the ponies out.

This is who everyone got:

Emily and Flame
? ? ? ? ?

Just for the
assessment. Flame's
beautiful, but I rea
want Emerald!

Chantelle and Charm

Elena and Jewel

Madison and Sugar

Frankie and Star

Morgan and Monsoon

Charlotte and Sparkle

Olivia and Tally
(her own pony!)

Neema and Prince

We all mounted up and rode out into the manège. As we began walking around the track, with Chantelle and Charm leading the way, I sat up nicely on Flame and tried to concentrate on riding really well to prove to Sally that I'm good enough to handle Emerald.

When we'd walked around on both reins and done a few circles and walk to halt transitions, Sally called out for each of us to trot to the back of the ride in turn. When it was my turn, Flame bucked and skittered sideways, and she wouldn't go into trot. I got a little flustered in case Sally thought I wasn't good for not making a nice transition, but then I made myself take a deep breath, get down into my seat, and steer Flame back onto the track. I took half the long side to get a really forward-going bouncy walk so that when I asked again, she trotted on without messing around. And it worked!

"Good girl, Emily!" Sally called out.

"Yeah, go, Ems!" whooped Frankie.

"Um, excuse me, who's the teacher here?" said Sally sternly, but she wasn't really angry.

Frankie giggled and I couldn't help smiling, too. I think maybe she truly is a really nice girl and not just nice to you when she feels like it.

The rest of the lesson went well, although Flame had a little bit of a freak-out when I asked for canter. But I kept calm and asked again at the next corner, and then we got it okay.

After the assessment, I was worried about not doing everything perfectly on Flame, but Sally smiled at me on the way back to the yard. She said she was impressed, but she just had to go and speak to Jason….

Oh, there she is….

Two mins later – I CAN ride Emerald!!!

I'm writing down Sally's exact words so I can remember them FOREVER.

She said,

"Flame really tested you today, and you kept calm and in control. You're not just a good rider, Emily, but you've got a really good understanding of ponies, too. I think you'll be okay to have Emerald as your pony this week."

Well, something like that, anyway!

I almost hugged her, but I didn't because she is the instructor. I couldn't stop beaming, though!

Gotta go—it's time to get down to the yard. I can't wait to see my GORGEOUS pony!

MY pony—hee hee.

I can't believe she's really mine.

Monday, after our second lesson

I'm so happy that I got to ride Emerald this afternoon! But the lesson didn't exactly go very well. After lunch, we gathered in the yard, and Sally read out which groups everyone would be in. They are:

Group B (my group)	Group A
Chantelle and Charm	Morgan and Monsoon
Elena and Jewel	Madison and Sugar
Charlotte and Sparkle	Neema and Prince
Olivia and Tally	Frankie and Star
* Emily and Emerald *	

Sally explained that she'll see how Emerald does in Group B, but that we might have to go into Group A for some lessons—like if my group's doing jumping, because she doesn't think Emerald would be able to cope with that. I said that was fine, and it was so great how Frankie grabbed my arm and said, "I hope you do come into Group A sometimes, Ems, 'cos then we can ride together!"

Then we had our lecture about tacking up, so we all got our ponies' stuff out of the tack room to practice on them in the barn. I went right up to Emerald, staggering under the weight of her saddle, with her bridle jangling on my shoulder, and accidentally scared her. Once I'd calmed her down, Lydia, who was teaching our lecture, called me over to the main pen to join in.

We learned about the different parts of the bridle and saddle and what types of bit there are, and Lydia demonstrated on Prince how to tack up properly. She also gave us some helpful tips for the difficult parts like getting the bit in, and she was really smiley and nice, even when we were having trouble.

Then when we got to do it for ourselves, Sally came and stood in the main pen with the others, while Lydia helped me with Emerald. I'm really glad she did because I didn't want Emerald to suddenly try and bolt off when I had the bridle half on.

As we led our ponies out into the yard, I could tell that Emerald was getting agitated about being around the others. She kept throwing her head in the air and startling at every tiny noise. I tried to stay calm and not panic, but it was tricky. I love Emerald so much already, and I didn't want to let her down by freaking out. Lydia held my reins for me while I mounted up and got my stirrups straightened out.

As soon as I was on, I found it easy to get a good seat because Emerald is so slim, and my legs seemed to fit around her in just the right place—see, I knew we were meant to be together!

But during the lesson, I couldn't help getting the feeling that she'd rather I was on the floor!

She was just about fine as we walked around the barn, although she did keep turning her head too much to the inside. I tried to pull it around, but Sally called out that I should relax and let Emerald find the bit in her own time. We were okay doing our walk/halt transitions, but as soon as we all trotted on as a ride, Emerald went bucking right across the middle of the manège to the other side of the track! Luckily, Sally called out to me to grab the pommel—otherwise, I would've gone flying off.

When Emerald finally stopped, Sally said, "Are you okay, Emily? Can you bring her back around past the others and ask for trot again? We can't let her get away with that."

I nodded, although when I took up the reins

again, my hands were shaking. I got Emerald to trot on, but it was a real battle to get her past everyone in a straight line because she wanted to go back over to the other side of the manège. When I finally got to the back of the ride with only one cut corner and two more little bucks, everyone said great job. I felt really embarrassed about them paying so much attention to me, but also very proud that they thought I'd done okay. Sally said, "Just keep handling Emerald the way you took charge of Flame this morning, and you'll be fine."

Emerald is much more of a challenge than Flame, though. We've got so many things to work on! But I hope that once we get used to each other, it'll improve.

As I walked her back into the barn to untack, I told her how well she'd done in a soft, gentle voice. After all, she'd tried her best. It's not her fault she's so nervous, poor thing! Sally says she came from this elderly lady who wasn't really well enough to take care of her and kept her in a little paddock on her own (and everyone knows ponies love company). And also that these kids used to go and tease her, chasing her around and trying to climb on her.

 THAT MAKES ME SO ANGRY! 

How could anyone treat a pony like that?!

At least it can't happen anymore. Thank goodness Sunnyside Stables rescued her from being lonely and scared. But it's not surprising that she finds it loud and a little unsettling here. Poor Emerald! I'll just have to work extra hard at proving to her that she can trust people—starting right now!

It's almost my turn in the shower, but I said I'd go last so I can quickly write this

Jason was just about to start our ping pong tournament when Sally poked her head around the game room door and asked if I wanted to help her turn Emerald out for the first time.

Well, of course I did! Any chance to spend more time with my pony!

But it didn't exactly work out in the end.

With Sally beside me, I walked Emerald up the road to the field. All the other ponies were already grazing as I led her through the gate and unclipped her lead rope. Then Sally and I leaned on the fence and watched.

Emerald didn't seem to know what to do. At first, she stood by the gate just eyeing the others nervously. Then when Sally encouraged her to go off, she bolted right up to Flame, who just chased her back across the field, squealing and bucking.

So poor Emerald ended up by herself again.

I felt like shouting to Flame, "Be nice to her! She doesn't know anyone and she's only trying to make friends with you!" But Sally explained that ponies have a sort of special code that new arrivals have to respect, and that Emerald was ignoring it.

"Well, she doesn't mean to," I grumbled. "It's not like she's trying to be horrible."

"No, of course not," said Sally. "But she's been on her own for so long that she might have forgotten, or maybe she was taken away from her mother too young, so she never learned these things in the first place. She doesn't understand how to fit in."

I felt even sorrier for Emerald then. I find it difficult to fit in, too, so I understand exactly how she feels!

Emerald tried to make friends with Flame a couple more times, but she kept getting chased away.

I felt really awful just watching—it reminded me of when Cindy at my old yard suddenly decided she didn't like me, and then her friends all followed her lead and wouldn't hang around with me, either.

Sally sighed. "This isn't going as well as I'd hoped," she said. "I think we'll have to stable Emerald for a while until she gets the hang of herd dynamics."

Of course I wanted my beautiful pony to join in with the others, but I could see that wasn't going to happen. And we couldn't leave her there feeling frightened and lonely all night. At least in a stable she'd be cozy and safe.

So Sally went into the field and caught her, and we got a nice deep bed ready in a spare stable in the main yard. I led Emerald in, and as I took off her head collar, I gave her a big kiss and hug and told her not to worry about the other ponies being meanies because I love her A LOT.

I kept finding excuses to stay with her, like filling her water bucket right up, double-checking her hooves for stones, and wiping invisible specks of dirt out of her eyes. Sally had to call me away in the end.

When I got back to the game room the ping pong tournament was half over, but I did get to join in the doubles 'cos Frankie asked me to go with her. We turned out to be pretty good against Olivia and Neema, and when we won Frankie held up her hand to do a high five. I did it back even though I was nervous about Chantelle and Charlie watching (I thought they might think I was acting like a big head). But they didn't seem bothered.

Oh, that's Olivia out of the shower, so I absolutely have to go in now, seeing as I'm the last one and I don't want to miss out on having my hot chocolate in the kitchen—yum!

Tuesday–I'm quickly writing this after lunch

This morning when I got into the yard, poor Emerald was hiding at the back of her stable, still really nervous and shy. I gave her a lot of attention, and then tied her up outside so I could muck out. While I was giving her a brush down, I had a good talk with her about how brave she was to try making friends with the other ponies last night.

Group B was jumping this morning, so we went in with Group A. Me and Frankie were really happy about being in the same group. First we warmed up in walk and trot and did a few changes of rein and turns and circles to get our ponies listening. Then Jess said we'd practice the gymkhana games we'll be doing on Friday.

Madison and Morgan were really excited

because they've never done a gymkhana before. Frankie started telling them all about the different games and how much fun they are, until Jess told her to stop chatting and concentrate on her riding! I've done a couple of gymkhana days, so I know a lot of the games, and also I was feeling pretty confident because Emerald had been so good during the warm-up—she even stayed calm when Madi and Sugar trotted to the back of the ride and came to a stop really close behind us.

But when we started practicing, Emerald fell apart. First we had to do the walk, trot, canter game. Me and Frankie went against each other, and she was great—instead of being competitive, she just did the walking up and trotting back really calmly so Emerald wouldn't get riled up. But even with Frankie and Star completely chilling out, when I asked for canter, Emerald bucked and went sideways, almost running into them.

I tensed up and squealed with fright, and of course that only made Emerald worse, so we had to give up on that game.

When Madi, Morgan, and Neema rode against each other, me and Frankie had to stand on the side. Poor Emerald wasn't comfortable with those three racing up and down in the same manège as her, and she kept trying to yank the reins out of my hands.

I think she would have been good at the weaving in and out of cones game if we'd done that first, but she was so wound up by then that she kept shooting out her hindquarters when we were bending around the cones. I did try to hold her in with my outside leg, but she ignored it and did her sideways prancing thing. I got really stressed out then, and I didn't enjoy the rest of the lesson, especially not when she bolted off while we were waiting for our turn in the relay race. ARGH!

When we were all untacking in the barn, Sally came over to me. Emerald was still in her separate pen, so I was on my own with her. Sally had noticed it hadn't gone too well, and I tried to act like everything was fine, but she could tell I was pretty upset. She even said I might have to miss the gymkhana on Friday if things don't improve A LOT.

And then she said the WORST thing, which was, "Emily, you can always swap back onto

Flame for the rest of the week, if you like. That doesn't mean you won't be able to spend time with Emerald, but you'll get more of a chance to focus on your own riding and development."

I felt all hot and flustered then, and I really hoped Emerald couldn't understand what she was saying.

I looked at my pony's gorgeous face and rubbed her neck. "No thanks, I'm fine," I muttered, hoping Sally wouldn't be too annoyed with me.

"No, I didn't think you'd want to," she said. "I do admire your loyalty and determination. But I'll have to think about how we can make this work so that you both get the best out of the week."

"Okay," I managed to mutter. "Thanks."

When she left, I gave Emerald a fierce hug. NOTHING is going to separate us!

At lunch, Frankie could tell I was still a little stressed out and she cheered me up in a typical Frankie-type way, which was by having a competition to see how many grapes we could get in our mouths at once. (I got 9 and she got 12, the big mouth!) We ended up laughing hysterically, and I do feel a little better now.

Oh, gotta go. Frankie wants me to go around with her and make a list of everyone's fave songs!

Tuesday before dinner,
but after our yard duties

Well, this afternoon Sally rearranged things so that me and Emerald could have a one-on-one lesson with her! So I had the lecture with Frankie's group (which was really fun, on points of the horse and colors and conformation), and then rode in the second manège while they had their lesson. That meant the Group B girls had to have their lecture on their own with Lydia. I thought they might be annoyed with me for making things change around, but actually they were happy 'cos it meant they got to ride right away after lunch—phew!

In the manège, Sally asked me to warm up Emerald by myself, and I felt really grown up deciding things like when to make transitions into halt and do turns and circles and go into trot.

After about 15 minutes, Sally called to me to halt at M and she came up and gave Emerald a pat. When she said how well we'd done in the warm-up, I couldn't help grinning with pride, and Emerald looked pretty pleased with herself, too. She definitely prefers being on our own to the group lessons! Then Sally said, "Okay then, let's get going. What do you think we need to work on?"

I said:

"I know we need to practice staying on the track in canter, and also Emerald needs to stop leaning on the inside rein when I'm trying to get her to bend on a circle, and I've got to stop her from shying every time we pass the gate and prancing about in walk, and when she charges off, I have to remember to use half halts and turns to stop her instead of panicking...."

I thought I was being really horsey by going into all that detail, but Sally just gave me an amused look. "Actually, there's only one main thing we need to work on," she said, "and it begins with 'C.'"

I stared at her, puzzled, and went,

I felt so silly when she said,

Of course! If we can both gain confidence, Emerald will calm down, and then a lot of our problems will improve naturally.

So we got to work. Sally kept reminding me to pay attention to the signals Emerald was giving, so that if she was getting too wound up in walk and threatening to take off, I could change direction or circle her or ask for a small section of trot. It was great, but not the kind of thing you can do in a group lesson. Like, you couldn't suddenly change direction without warning everyone!

As the lesson was ending, we had a little bit of a disaster, though. Jess opened the gate of the other manège to let Group A out, and when she shut it, it kind of clanged and Emerald went charging off again and bucked across the manège. I forgot all the confidence stuff we'd been learning and just grabbed the reins and stiffened up.

When Emerald finally came to a stop, my heart was absolutely pounding. It really hit me how much work we still have to do before we'll even be able to fit in with Group A, and I think we can forget about taking part in the gymkhana. I felt very disheartened, but Sally was firm and told me we just have to keep going, one step at a time. Then she got us to do some nice trot and canter transitions on a circle so we'd end on a good note.

Afterward, I walked Emerald around on a long rein to cool down 'cos we were both boiling! As Sally held the gate for me (being careful not to let it clang!), she said, "We're doing well, but I think I know someone who can help us do even better. How would you feel about missing the carriage-driving trip tomorrow?"

"To be with Emerald?" I asked. Sally nodded, and I instantly said it was fine. The more time I can spend with my fabulous pony, the better!

Sally didn't explain anymore. Instead she just smiled and said, "Okay, let me see what I can arrange. And great job today."

I thanked her and took Emerald back to her pen to untack and brush her down. As I was a little late finishing, the Group A girls had untacked already, and Group B was mucking out the barn, chatting away. Then Charlie laughed really loudly at something Elena said and made poor Emerald jump. I rubbed her nose and whispered, "It's okay, Em—you don't need to be scared anymore. It's different here."

Saying that made me think about myself, too. I'm like Emerald, jumping at every little thing—I'm always expecting the older girls to suddenly not like me. But the fact is that they haven't done anything except be nice.

Then I thought about how Frankie has been such a good friend, and I suddenly realized that I'm starting to trust her, just like Emerald is starting to trust me.

"It really is different here, Em," I whispered again. "For both of us."

Wednesday, early in the morning before the others are awake

Last night, me and Frankie made a secret camp by hanging our towels down from her bunk across to mine so you couldn't see in. It was so cool! We did try and get Olivia to come in with us, too, but she was so sound asleep that we couldn't wake her up!

Frankie brought out this big pink tub, which was full of yummy things for a midnight party, and soon we were whispering jokes to each other, and scarfing down gummy bears and jellybeans and chips (we were giggling so much 'cos we had to suck them instead of crunching so that Jess wouldn't hear us!). It was really fun, like having a sleepover.

I hope Frankie will come for a real sleepover at my new house, like next week or something. I think she will if I ask her 'cos we've become really good friends—and she lives in the same town that we've just moved to! In fact, we've gotten so close that I started telling her something more serious, about what happened in my old yard with the older girls.

It was Frankie who called it bullying.

I hadn't really thought of it like that, but actually, she's right.

I told her everything—about how Cindy and her friends used to act as if they owned the yard and made me do all the horrible jobs, like poop picking the field and scrubbing the feed and water buckets. And how they did all the nice stuff like grooming the ponies and tacking up ready for people's lessons. And then I told Frankie the worst thing of all—about the way they went quiet when I came into the tack room or wherever, like they'd been talking about me. Then Cindy used to say stuff to me like, "Yes, can we help you?" and I always turned bright red and wished I could become invisible and melt away. It made me upset even thinking about what happened. Frankie put her arm around me then.

"I bet you think I'm really wimpy," I said, but she went, "No way! 'Course I don't think that! I think you were brave to keep going there when they were so awful—it shows how much you love ponies! Anyway, the yard staff should have been keeping an eye out for bullying, and they didn't. That was wrong." She frowned at me and added, "You should've told someone."

I shrugged. Maybe for someone like Frankie that would've been easy, but I'm just so shy.

But I loved that she was so angry with Cindy and her group. She really is a true friend.

Later on, we were talking about schools, and we figured out that I'm going to be in the same class as her at Westbrooke Elementary when school starts! Frankie started telling me all about her friends and the different teachers and the lunchtime clubs you can do. Anyway, we completely forgot about being quiet! Frankie started doing an impression of this teacher named Mr. Gregory, who's like a mad scientist, and it made us both laugh so much we had to stuff our fists in our mouths to stop the noise from coming out.

Too late, though. The next thing we knew, Jess was coming up the stairs! Frankie vaulted onto her bunk and scrambled under the covers. We were both pretending to be asleep, but we couldn't stop ourselves from giggling into our pillows. Frankie did this big fake snore and that made me laugh even more. Jess strongly whispered to us to go to sleep, but she didn't seem really angry (phew!).

Oh, it's so cool here at Pony Camp! Everyone's so nice, and I've made a good friend and got the pony of my dreams! I'm really looking forward to spending the whole day with Emerald tomorrow! I wonder what Sally has lined up for us. I can't wait to find out!

Wednesday, after the most amazing time!

The others aren't back from the carriage-driving trip yet, and I did offer to do extra yard duties in my spare time, but Sally said I'd earned a break. So I went upstairs to get this diary, and now I'm sitting outside in the sunshine, writing! I've had the most amazing day with Emerald. We've both learned so much—and had a ton of fun, too!

Emerald was hiding at the back of her stable when I arrived this morning, but as soon as she saw me, she came up for a hug. After the others had set off on the trip, Sally asked me to help Lydia in the yard. Then, about half an hour later, she called me over to the parking lot.

A dusty old orange pickup truck, with a wild mustang painted on the hood, was pulling up. My heart was hammering as this huge man climbed out wearing chaps, a blue checked shirt, and a cowboy hat. He looked scary from the back, but as soon as he turned around, I knew he was really nice.

He gave me a big smile, then lifted Sally off the ground in a hug and said, "Mr. Bob at your service, ma'am." It was funny 'cos he didn't have a midwestern accent, as I'd expected.

First of all, Mr. Bob asked me to bring Emerald into the manège wearing only her head collar. I'd thought I'd be riding right away, but Mr. Bob said, "We need to get Emerald to trust you, and the best place for that is on the ground."

Mr. Bob put Emerald on this really long lead rope, sort of like a lunge rein, and got her to walk around one way and then the other in a circle. Then he let me have a turn. My circle was a lot less smooth than his to start with, but after a while, Emerald stopped weaving in and out and went steadily around.

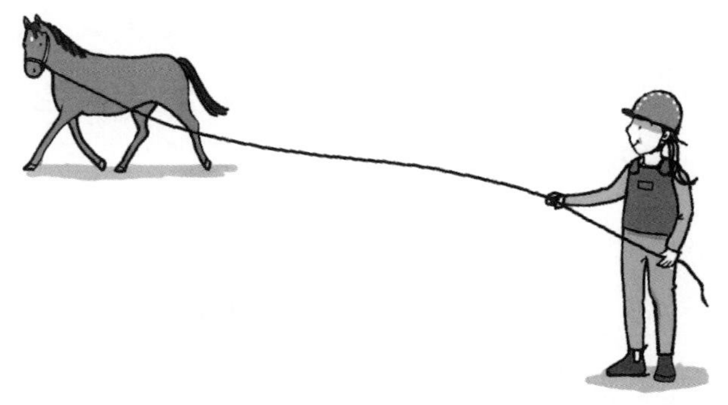

We did the same in trot, and then Mr. Bob got me to walk around wherever I wanted at the end of the rope and to let Emerald just follow me—I was amazed when she actually did! Then he showed me how to wiggle the rope a little to get her to go backward. At first she was confused, but she soon got the hang of it.

Then, when I thought I was finally going to ride, Mr. Bob said, "Now, let's give you two a little free time together." I didn't really know what he meant, but then he took the lead rope off Emerald and let her hang out with me in the manège, doing whatever she wanted. And it was so cool that what she wanted to do was follow me around! So we took a walk one way and then the other, and then I tried jogging and she trotted next to me.

Then she took a trot around and I followed her. She finished off with a snort and a roll in the woodchips. I didn't copy that, of course!

"Good job, Miss Emily," Mr. Bob said as I walked back to the gate, and Sally was smiling, too. She said it was time for a break then—I felt really grown up that it was just me and the two adults, even though they had coffee and I had orange juice. When Mr. Bob asked me how Pony Camp was going, I felt shy at first, but soon I started chatting away about Emerald and Frankie and all the other girls and ponies. I even ended up telling him about our secret midnight feast!

When it was time to ride, Sally and I gave Emerald a brush down and tacked up, and soon I was out in the manège on my gorgeous pony. And guess what? Sally was riding, too, on her horse, Blue. She said it would help Emerald get used to being with other ponies in the manège.

Mr. Bob had a different style of teaching than Sally. He wanted us to focus on staying relaxed and in tune with our ponies (well, pony and horse!). We had to let our hips and legs go a bit looser and more relaxed, and move with our horses' rhythm. He got us to exaggerate it so much at first that we felt like floppy dolls! When Sally trotted to the back of the ride and came up behind us, I thought for a moment that Emerald was going to freak out, but she didn't. All that work we'd done on the ground really had paid off!

After about 20 minutes we were nicely warmed up, and Mr. Bob asked me if there was anything special I wanted to work on. I said, "Not really. I'm just happy if Emerald's happy...." I trailed off, but his smile encouraged me to be brave. "It would be great if Emerald and I could join in the gymkhana on Friday," I said then. "But only if it's the right thing for her."

Mr. Bob agreed to give it a try, and soon me and Sally were doing the walk, trot, canter race, and the weaving through cones one, and Emerald really did enjoy it!

Then Sally said we should make it more realistic and called to Lydia and her friend Paula to tack up Fly (Lydia's liver chestnut horse) and Rusty, one of the riding school horses. At first, with four of us tearing up and down the manège, I really thought Emerald was going to freak out, but she did okay. She got pretty frazzled when we were doing the relay race, though, because I had to ride her very close to Paula and Rusty, but I stayed calm and helped her keep it together.

Sally said afterward how well we'd done, but that in the real gymkhana it will be even more difficult, with people cheering and more ponies in the manège. She said she'd leave it up to me whether we wanted to just do some of the games on Friday and added that we didn't have to join in at all if I felt that Emerald wouldn't like it. It was great that she was letting me judge for myself what was right for us. It made me feel like we're really a team.

Afterward, I tied Emerald up in the yard and gave her a thorough head-to-hoof groom, and Sally let me wash her tail and then braid it so it would dry all wavy! Then she came with me while I took Emerald for a walk up and down the road. I thought we might turn her out into the field with the other ponies, but Sally said we should probably give her one more day. So my little Emerald is all cozy in her stable now, tired out and very pleased with herself. I can't believe how much I love her after only three days!

Oh, the van has just pulled up. I hope the others had a good time—but, ugh, I just had a horrible thought—what if Frankie has gotten really friendly with someone else after today and she doesn't want to hang around with me anymore? GULP! I really hope not!

Wednesday, after swimming

Well, I was just being silly about Frankie (phew!). It sounds like they all had a great time on the carriage-driving trip, though. They each had a ride in a carriage pulled by a pony named Bayleaf. And they saw all these beautiful ponies and horses and different carriages, and they sat in this really grand one from Victorian times that's actually been on TV.

It sounded like fun, but I still didn't mind missing it because I got to spend the day with Emerald. Frankie said she wished I'd come, but that she wasn't lonely 'cos she hung around with her sister and the older girls. Then she said, "You are coming on the hack tomorrow, though, aren't you?" And I went, "What hack?"

Frankie said Jess told them about it in the van. Both groups are going together for a long ride through the countryside, with a picnic lunch halfway. I really want to go and I'm sure Emerald can handle it, as long as I stay calm and focused. But I'll have to see what Sally thinks.

At dinnertime, all the girls were chattering away about the trip. Because I didn't go I felt kind of left out, and I was tempted to just fade into the background. But something, maybe seeing Emerald's courage in the lessons with Mr. Bob today, made me try to join in. I asked a few questions, and everyone was really excited to talk to me about it.

Then Elena asked me how *my* day was, and at that moment everyone seemed to have finished talking and they were all paying attention to *me*. I blushed and that old feeling of wanting to turn invisible came back, but then I thought, *If Emerald can be brave, so can I*. And once I started talking about Emerald, I got pulled along with excitement about what we'd done and how far she'd come today.

Then Morgan started telling a story, and I was just sitting there thinking, *Wow, did I actually have everyone listening to me and being really interested?*

That made me feel so happy, and when we went swimming this evening, I went and joined in doing handstands on the bottom of the pool and having races and playing water volleyball without even *thinking* that I was joining in. That's amazing for me!

So it's not just Emerald who has gained a lot of confidence with Sally and Mr. Bob's help. I have, too!

Gotta go—Frankie's saying hurry up 'cos my hot chocolate's getting cold!

Thursday, after our lecture on road safety and first aid and what to do if you get lost (fingers crossed THAT won't happen!)

Sally said me and Emerald can go on the picnic ride with everyone else. YAY! When I went to muck Em out this morning, she was looking out of her stable door, waiting for me! How great is that! I was so happy, and I gave her a huge hug. I started to feel a little upset then, though, because tomorrow is the last day of Pony Camp. I know that paying for this vacation was a big stretch for Mom and there's no way I'll be able to come here for lessons during the school year, so it will be the end of Em & Em.

Still, feeling sad made me more determined to enjoy every second I have left with my beautiful pony. I'm off down to the yard now to tack up, and Lydia's going to show us how to bandage our ponies' legs because we'll be going through the woods, and we might come across some prickly bushes.

Thursday still, but after the picnic ride—well, me and Emerald had the most amazing (and scary!) adventure today

Me and Frankie have figured out that we did about two and a half hours' riding this afternoon—no wonder we are so tired! We made sure our ponies had fresh water when we got in and gave them a brush down in the barn, but Sally said we didn't have to do our usual TONS of yard work because we were all so completely flaked out from the long, hot ride. Instead, she let us go swimming to cool off! It was so refreshing diving into the water and splashing around.

So now we've dried off and gotten dressed, and me and Frankie are writing in our Pony Camp Diaries. We're sitting on the platform thing overlooking the manèges (not that there's any riding to watch at the moment, but it's a nice place to hang out).

When we were tacking up our ponies for the ride, Lydia showed us how to put their head collars on under their bridles. I thought it was a little strange at first, but she explained that while we were having our picnic, we could slip the bridles off so they could munch on the grass!

Jason, Sally, and Lydia all came with us—Sally was riding Blue and Lydia was on Fly, who is seriously speedy!

We all rode in single file up the road. Sally told me to wedge Emerald in behind Prince and Neema because:

a. Prince wouldn't spook if Emerald jumped at something

and

b. he'd stop her from charging off.

We were all walking along in the sunshine, then we turned up a track and had a little trot and it was just so awesome! We rode for a while through some woods, and I was a little worried that Emerald would spook at the low branches, but she didn't. In fact, as we walked up this path by the edge of the fields, I was thinking we'd finally cracked it and that she was completely cured of her flighty behavior—ha ha, silly me!

Suddenly, this pheasant flew out of a bush beside Emerald and she totally freaked out. She went skittering sideways while bucking her legs in the air, and I was so surprised I just fell right off. I found myself lying on the ground, my heart pounding with shock, listening to her hooves thundering away across the stubble field.

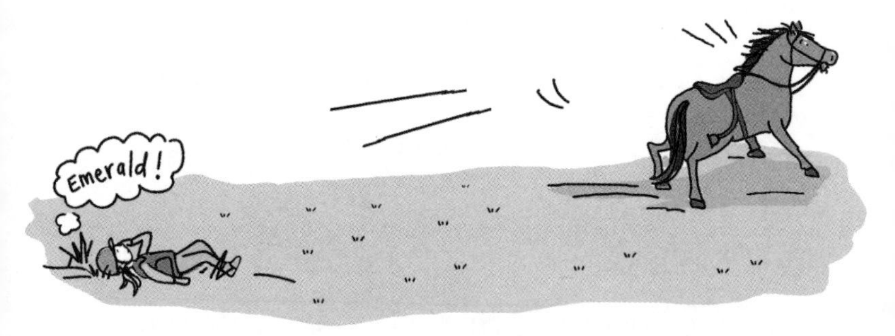

Sally dismounted and handed Blue's reins to someone else (maybe it was Lydia). She crouched beside me and asked if I was okay, but all I could think about was Emerald. I staggered to my feet and went running across the field after her.

"Emily, wait!" Jason called out, but I heard Sally say, "She won't listen. Don't worry, I'll go." Then she came chasing after me.

When I reached the top of the hill, I saw Emerald at the far end of the field. She was pacing up and down with her tail swishing. I started to run toward her, but Sally caught up with me. "Go steady," she panted, "or she'll take off. Just get a little closer, and then wait for her to come to you."

I blinked at her. I'd been expecting her to scold me for ignoring Jason and then send me straight back to the group. But instead she was going to let me try and catch Emerald. I knew I had to be really slow and careful. If she went charging off again, she could run into the road, or trip and hurt herself.

I walked down the hill, making sure to stay in Emerald's sight so I didn't spook her. Then I stopped, a little ways away. She eyed me suspiciously at first and shifted from hoof to hoof. After we'd both stood still for a long time, I started to worry that she was never going to come to me. I glanced around and saw everyone standing on the brow of the hill, watching, and I started panicking that we were holding up the whole ride and that they'd all be annoyed. I think that's why I tried something careless. I lunged forward and made a grab for Emerald's rein.

But she whinnied and skittered away.

I felt flustered and frustrated. "Oh, Emerald, come on!" I cried. I didn't want to turn around and look at Sally 'cos I thought she'd scold me and take over. But I didn't know what to do next.

Then I remembered what Mr. Bob had taught me.

I couldn't worry about what the others would think. I had to be patient. I had to let Emerald come to me.

So I stood, and I stood, and I stood. "It's okay, Em," I said quietly. "You can trust me. And we'll just stay here for as long as you need."

Somehow, Emerald seemed to understand, because after a while she gave me a shy glance, and then another, and then she loped toward me, her neck loose and relaxed. I gave her a big pat and rubbed her neck, while gently lifting her reins down over her head. Then I crossed her stirrups over and led her back toward Sally.

"I'm so proud of you, Emerald," I whispered.

When we reached the others, Sally gave me a leg-up and off we went again. Instead of being annoyed with me, everyone was chattering about how well I'd done! Of course, me being me, I got embarrassed about being the center of attention, and I couldn't help feeling all red and flustered. But it wasn't in a bad way this time. I didn't want to become invisible. Instead, I felt proud. Of me and of Emerald—Em & Em, the super team! I sat up a little taller, and I couldn't help grinning. Now I know Emerald really does trust me, and that together, we can achieve anything!

Jess met us at the picnic site in the truck and handed out sandwiches, fruit, and some wonderfully cold cartons of orange juice. We clipped the ponies' lead ropes onto their head collars, took the bridles off, and let them graze while we ate

and chatted (although Emerald was much more interested in my ham and cheese sandwich than the grass!). There was no bathroom, so we had to hold each other's ponies while we went in the bushes! It was so funny having to do that and we couldn't stop giggling. I held Sugar for Madi, and this time Emerald didn't seem to mind standing that close to her—she really is making progress!

We rode a different way back to the yard, and Sally let us all have a canter up this stubble field. It was awesome! Olivia and Tally took off really fast, and only Lydia and Fly overtook them. I would've loved a seriously fast gallop, but I knew it wouldn't be good for Emerald to get that worked up (I wanted to be sure she'd stop again!), so I tucked her in behind Sugar and

Monsoon and had a gentle canter to the top. She really enjoyed it and easily came back to a nice springy trot when I asked.

In fact, she did great the whole way back. We even had to walk through this river, and it wasn't that deep, but she got a little spooked by the shadows on the water. Instead of panicking, I just stuck closely behind Sally and followed Blue across without even looking down. Before Emerald knew it, we were on the other side.

Oh, and now Jess is calling us in because me and Frankie are up for setting the table and helping get dinner ready. Better go!

Thursday, just before lights out

Well, I didn't think I could get any prouder of Emerald after the picnic ride, but I am now! We had a movie night tonight, and we were all watching *Spirit* and eating popcorn (yum!) when Sally popped her head around the game room door and called me over. I was worried for a minute that I'd done something wrong, but in fact she wanted me to come up to the field with her and try turning Emerald out with the other ponies again. I asked if Frankie could come, too, and Sally said okay, so we all collected Emerald from the barn and walked up to the field.

The sun was just starting to go down and everything was glowing golden, and the smell of grass and dry dirt and Emerald was all around me. Being out there with my great instructor and my new friend and my fabulous pony was just the best feeling ever, and I had to push away the thought that tomorrow Pony Camp is coming to an end.

Sally let me walk Emerald into the field and take off her lead rope. I gave her a big pat and whispered in her ear, "Go on, be brave. If I can make new friends, I know you can, too." Then I gave her mane a final ruffle and walked away.

I hitched myself up onto the fence with Sally and Frankie, and we all watched.

At first Emerald just stood there, and I felt a knot in my stomach and a lump in my throat. I so desperately wanted to see her fit in—I just wished I could go and make friends for her!

She stood still for a while longer, and then, slowly, she began to wander around the group in a big circle, staying quite a ways away from them. I kept expecting her to charge at them like she had before, but she didn't (phew!). Instead, she walked in smaller and smaller circles around Flame, Sparkle, and Charm as the other ponies moved off to graze farther away.

She kept circling closer and closer, and I looked at Sally because I was worried she was about to get chased away like last time and maybe even kicked. But Sally smiled at me and said, "Almost there. Watch."

And then the most amazing thing happened.

Flame kind of shifted so that she was standing sideways to Emerald, and Emerald went up to her. I held my breath because I thought the others would definitely chase her then, but they didn't seem bothered. Flame nudged Emerald around a bit and Emerald just let her, and then suddenly they were all grazing together, and it looked like Emerald had always belonged there.

I felt all this happiness bubble up inside me, along with sadness that tomorrow I'll have to say good-bye to her. Sally squeezed my arm and said, "Great job, Emily. You helped her to do that, you know."

"Oh, I—" I began, but Frankie cut me off.

"Yeah, great job, Ems! You're like a total horse whisperer or something!" she said, grinning.

As we walked down the road, Frankie linked arms with me, and when we got back to the game room, the others were so curious about what we'd been up to that Olivia had to pause the movie so we could tell them all about Emerald joining the ponies in the field. Well, Frankie, being Frankie, did most of the talking and me, being me, blushed when she told them how Sally said I'd helped Emerald have the confidence to become part of the group.

Then I sat down and Neema put her legs on my lap and Madi asked me to braid her hair. Somehow, I don't think I'll wish I was invisible ever again. There is one thing I do wish, though—I wish that Pony Camp would never end and that I could keep coming to Sunnyside Stables and seeing Emerald forever and ever!

Friday—back in my new room in our new house. I've got the most AMAZING news!

Well, when I saw Sally talking to Mom while we were getting ready for the gymkhana, I had no idea that they were saying anything much. But it turns out that they were saying something very, VERY important, which I will reveal in a minute!

First of all, I just want to quickly write about how well Emerald did in the gymkhana. We all spent a long time making our ponies look nice for it and cleaning our tack.

When I finished, Emerald looked like this:

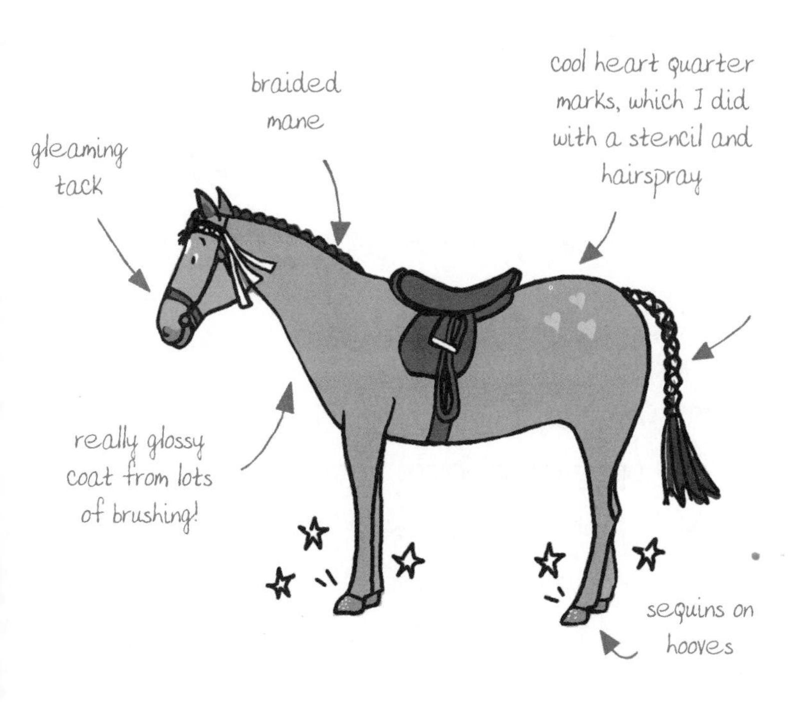

It was great to see Mom again. Of course, she fell totally in love with Emerald, and she was so surprised at me talking away about our lessons, and the picnic ride, and Frankie and the other girls, and Sally and Mr. Bob, instead of being quiet like I usually am.

I'd decided with Sally before the gymkhana that I'd join in with Group A's races, but only some of them.

So, me and Emerald did:

Walk, trot, canter

Weaving around the cones

Ball and bucket race

Apple bobbing

But we missed out on the relay and the bale stepping stones races because I thought she'd find those too spooky. I managed to keep her in check during our races, even though it meant that in the apple bobbing I stayed in trot when the others cantered up to the buckets. Amazingly, we actually won the walk, trot, canter against Frankie and Olivia—Emerald's speed when I did let her go meant we passed even super-fast Tally at the post!

After both groups had had their gymkhana games, everyone played Chase Me Charlie. Well, all except us. As I hadn't tried any jumping with Emerald, a competition with everyone watching didn't seem like a great place to start, so I led her off into the barn for a rest.

When I got back, I leaned on the fence next to Mom to watch the rest of the jumping. Jason was in charge with Sally helping, and when she saw me, she came over and said great job for handling the gymkhana games.

"Without you, Emerald wouldn't have achieved the amazing things she has," she said, and I suddenly realized that without Sally, me and Emerald wouldn't have achieved anything at all! In fact, we wouldn't even have been together! I said thanks to her for believing in me and giving me the chance to have Emerald as my pony for the week, and for rearranging the lessons for me and getting Mr. Bob to help us and, well, everything! Then I added, "I was worried you were going to take me off her, though!"

Sally smiled and said, "I did think about it. But I felt that you and Emerald were right for each other. You've taught each other what you needed to learn most—confidence. Funny how the things ponies have to teach us are sometimes not about technique or even about riding at all!"

I felt a big wave of love for Emerald then, and after that an even bigger wave of sadness that I'd have to leave her. I'd pushed it to the back of my mind so I could enjoy my last day, but just then the full force of having to say good-bye hit me, and tears sprang into my eyes. I was just about to rush off to the barn to spend every single moment I had left at Pony Camp with her (and probably cry a LOT!), when Sally said casually, "Oh, it's such a shame.

One of my best school-time helpers has just moved away. The yard's going to be such a mess without her."

I hardly dared to ask in case she said no, but I knew I had to take the chance. "I'd like to volunteer, and I bet Frankie would, too, if you think we'd be good enough," I managed to mumble. I looked up nervously.

"I think you'd both be great!" she said. And I had to duck under the fence and give her a hug, even though she's the instructor! Then I looked at Mom and she was beaming—turns out Sally had already cleared it with her (so that's what they were talking about!).

For a moment this horrible thought flashed through my head that maybe there would be older girls helping in the yard, too, who'd be horrible to me, but I know it's not like that here.

Then Sally said something even more amazing, which was, "Emerald will need some consistency and won't be suitable as a riding school pony for a long time yet, so if you can ride her every couple of days, you'll be helping her, too. And we'll keep working with Mr. Bob to really get her settled."

I was just absolutely staring at her, grinning. I said thank you a ton of times, but even if I'd said it a million times, it wouldn't have seemed like enough. Sally said it was enough after about 23 times, though!

After that, I still wanted Frankie to win the Chase Me Charlie, but I also wanted her to be out right away so I could tell her the incredible news! (She came in third in the end, after Chantelle and Charlie.)

Of course, it was still sad when Pony Camp was over, because us girls won't be together anymore. Morgan and Madison were both in tears about leaving their ponies, so the rest of us did our best to cheer them up. We got the moms and dads to take tons of pictures of us all squashed onto the bench, sitting on each other's laps and stuff. When I remember how I didn't dare join in with sitting on the bench at first, I can hardly believe it now! Without even thinking about being shy, I just plonked myself down onto Chantelle's lap. She was yelling, "OW, my legs!" and everyone was giggling and leaning on each other. Mom took a picture of us on my camera. I haven't downloaded it yet, but here's my drawing of what we looked like:

I'm seeing Emerald on Tuesday for a one-on-one session with Sally, but I still said a big good-bye to her and gave her tons of hugs and kisses and rubs and pats because I'll miss her so much until then. Then I pinned the first place rosette to her bridle so Mom could take a picture of us, and she looked so proud of herself.

Wow, it's amazing how much me and Emerald have helped each other this week, and it's even more amazing that it's only the beginning of our partnership!

I feel like the luckiest girl in the world—I've made a true friend in Frankie and found a beautiful stable yard where we can both help out in return for rides, and met an amazing instructor, but best of all I've teamed up with the most beautiful, wonderful, special pony! I just know it's going to be …

PONY CAMP diaries

Learn all about the world of ponies!

Glossary

Bending—directing the horse to ride correctly around a curve

Bit—the piece of metal that goes inside the horse's mouth. Part of the bridle.

Chase Me Charlie—a show jumping game where the jumps get higher and higher

Currycomb—a comb with rows of metal teeth used to clean (to curry) a pony's coat

Dandy brush—a brush with hard bristles that removes the dirt, hair, and any other debris stirred up by the currycomb

Frog—the triangular soft part on the underside of the horse's hoof. It's very important to clean around it with a hoof pick.

Girth—the band attached to the saddle and buckled around the horse's barrel to keep the saddle in place

Grooming—the daily cleaning and caring for the pony to keep them healthy and make them beautiful for competitions. A full grooming includes brushing your horse's coat, mane, and tail and picking out the hooves.

Gymkhana—a fun event full of races and other competitions

Hands—a way to measure the height of a horse

Glossary

Mane—the long hair on the back of a horse's neck. Perfect for braiding!

Manège—an enclosed training area for horses and their riders

Numnah—a piece of material that lies under the saddle and stops it from rubbing against the horse's back

Paces—a pony has four main paces, each made up of an evenly repeated sequence of steps. From slowest to quickest, these are the walk, trot, canter, and gallop.

Plodder—a slow, reliable horse

Pommel—the raised part at the front of the saddle

Pony—a horse under 14.2 hands in height

Rosette—a rose-shaped decoration with ribbons awarded as a prize! Usually, a certain color matches where you are placed during the competition.

Stirrups—foot supports attached to the sides of a horse's saddle

Tack—the main pieces of the pony's equipment, including the saddle and bridle. Tacking up a horse means getting them ready for riding.

Pony Colors

Ponies come in all ***colors****. These are some of the most common!*

Bay—Bay ponies have rich brown bodies and black manes, tails, and legs.

Black—A true black pony will have no brown hairs, and the black can be so pure that it looks a bit blue!

Chestnut—Chestnut ponies have reddish-brown coats that vary from light to dark red with no black points.

Dun—A dun pony has a sandy-colored body, with a black mane, tail, and legs.

Gray—Gray ponies come in a range of color varieties, including dapple gray, steel gray, and rose gray. They all have black skin with white, gray, or black hair on top.

Palomino—Palominos have a sandy-colored body with a white or cream mane and tail. Their coats can range from pale yellow to bright gold!

Piebald—Piebald ponies have a mixture of black-and-white patches—like a cow!

Skewbald—Skewbald ponies have patches of white and brown.

Pony Markings

As well as the main body color, many ponies also have white ***markings*** *on their faces and legs!*

On the legs:

Socks—run up above the fetlock but lower than the knee. The fetlock is the joint several inches above the hoof.

Stockings—extend to at least the bottom of the horse's knee, sometimes higher

On the face:

Blaze—a wide, straight stripe down the face from in between the eyes to the muzzle

Snip—a white marking on the pony's muzzle, between the nostrils

Star—a white marking between the eyes

Stripe—the same as a blaze but narrower

White/bald face—a very wide blaze that goes out past the eyes, making most of the pony's face look white!

Fan-tack-stic Cleaning Tips!

*Get your **tack** shining in no time with these top tips!*

- Clean your tack after every use, if you can. Otherwise, make sure you at least rinse the bit under running water and wash off any mud or sweat from your girth after each ride.
- The main things you will need are:
  — bars of saddle soap
  — a soft cloth
  — a sponge
  — a bottle of leather conditioner 
- As you clean your bit, check that it has no sharp edges and isn't too worn.
- Use a bridle hook or saddle horse to hold your bridle and saddle as you clean them. If you don't have a saddle horse, you can hang a blanket over a gate to put the saddle on. Avoid hanging your bridle on a single hook or nail because the leather might crack!

- Make sure you look carefully at the bridle before undoing it so that you know how to put it back together!
- Use the conditioner to polish the leather of the bridle and saddle and make them sparkle!
- Check under your numnah before you clean it. If the dirt isn't evenly spread on both sides, you might not be sitting evenly as you ride.
- Polish your metalwork occasionally. Cover the leather parts around it with a cloth and only polish the rings—not the mouthpiece, because that would taste horrible!

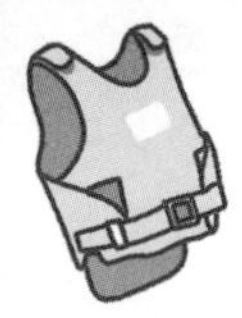

Going the Distance!

Find out how much you know about cross-country riding with this fun quiz! Can you go the distance?

1. For safety, the rider must wear:

a. A body warmer
b. A body protector
c. Full body armor

2. Cross-country boots can be worn by your pony to:

a. Look stylish
b. Make them go faster
c. Protect their legs from knocks

3. "Narrow," "angled," and "corner" are all types of:

a. Events
b. Fences
c. Ditches

4. Cross-country riding differs from racing, as your pony should never finish:

a. Exhausted
b. Hungry
c. Angry

5. Cross country forms part of three day eventing competitions, along with:

a. Showjumping and racing
b. Showjumping and dressage
c. Dressage and dressing-up

6. A cross-country rider usually wears a:

a. Skull cap
b. Skeleton cap
c. Shower cap

7. All cross-country courses are designed to:

a. Look the same
b. Look different
c. Look exciting but a little scary

8. An advanced water combination includes a number of:

a. Riders and routes
b. Riders and fences
c. Fences and routes

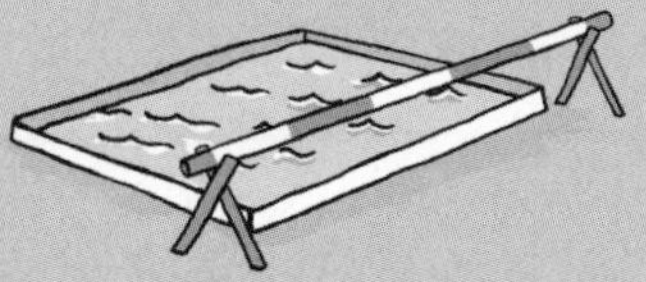

Answers: 1.b, 2.c, 3.b, 4.a, 5.b, 6.a, 7.b, 8.c

Beautiful Braids!

Follow this step-by-step guide to give your pony a perfect tail braid!

1. Start at the very top of the tail and take two thin bunches of hair from either side, braiding them into a strand in the center.

2. Continue to pull in bunches from either side and braid down the center of the tail.

3. Keep braiding like this, making sure you're pulling the hair tightly to keep the braid from unraveling!

4. When you reach the end of the dock—where the bone ends—stop taking in bunches from the side but keep braiding downward until you run out of hair.

5. Fasten with a braid band!

Gymkhana Ready!

Get your pony looking spectacular for the gymkhana with these grooming ideas!

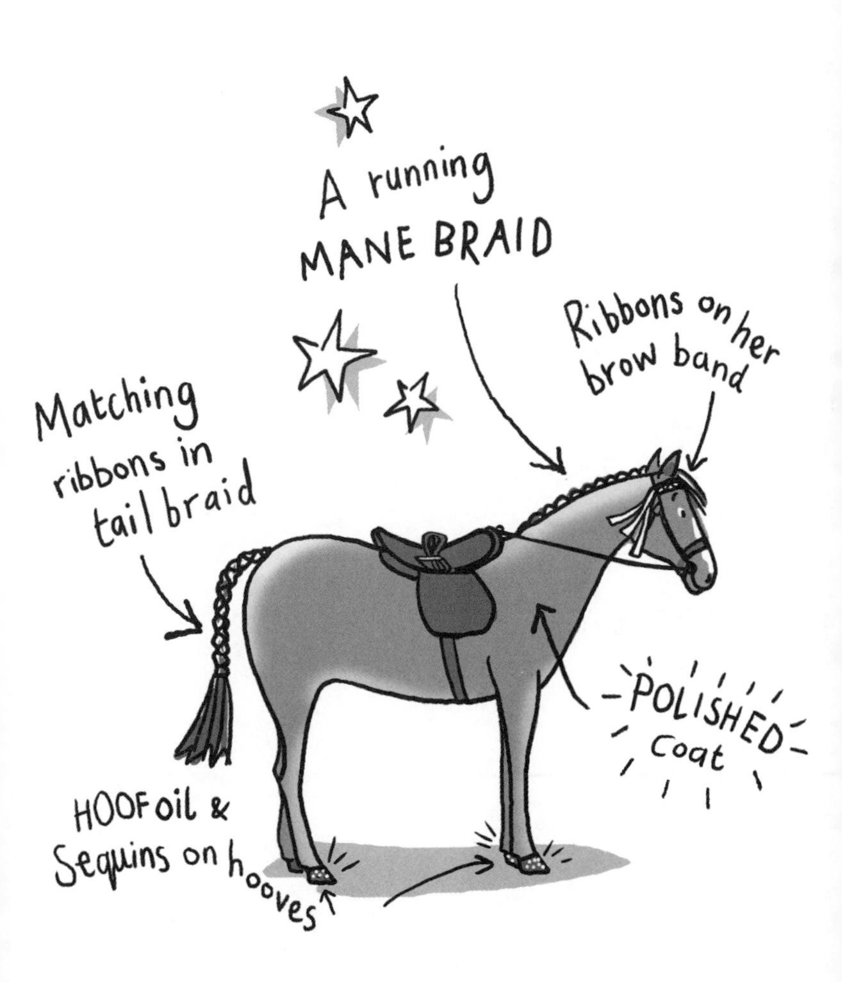

Turn the page for a sneak peek at another story in the series!

Monday, after lunch

Well, here I am at Pony Camp, and Jess has given me this special diary to write all about it!

It's amazing here, with so many ponies and two manèges and a swimming pool! And the girls are really nice, too. I just wish that Apple was here to enjoy it with me. She's my pony … well, I mean, she was my pony, but I got too big to ride her, and Mom and Dad said they had to sell her. That was 1 month, 23 days and, um, 5 hours ago. And I haven't ridden since—well, I hadn't until this morning, anyway. I found it really strange being on a pony again, and I was sad that it wasn't Apple.

When I got here, other cars were pulling up. Girls tumbled out, chattering excitedly and dragging big suitcases into the farmhouse.

I was feeling nervous, so I stayed close to Mom when she went to register me in the office. I wish I hadn't, though, because she was doing that annoying thing of talking about me as if I'm not there, saying "Cassie" this and "she" that.

She was telling Sally the instructor and Lydia (one of the stable girls) about me not riding since they sold Apple. Well, actually, she said, "since we sold Apple," and I said, "since you did" because I had nothing to do with it—I would never have given up my beautiful pony! Then she said how I won't even go back to the stables where I used to keep Apple, and how I've lost touch with my riding friends because I always said no to going up there with them and after a while they stopped asking me.

Apple

I was getting really upset and annoyed, and

I think Sally noticed 'cos she sent me off into the farmhouse to unpack and meet the other girls. Lydia walked up there with me, and on the way, she squeezed my shoulders and said, "Don't worry, Cassie—you'll be okay at Sunnyside." That was so nice of her, but it also almost made me start crying.

When I got to the room. I started unpacking right away to take my mind off Apple. I could hear girls chatting in the other rooms, but mine was empty. The bed by the window was unmade and covered in clothes and magazines, but the bunk beds looked free, so I took the top one.

After a few minutes, Mom came up to say good-bye because she had to go to work. She and Dad are always really busy at their offices, and my big brother, Henry, is away this week, too, on a hiking trip with some friends. He loves canoeing over waterfalls and stuff like that. I used to be outdoorsy, too, and I practically lived at the stables while Apple was there! But when she was sold, I ended up moping around in my room, not really knowing what to do with myself. Mom and Dad tried to talk to me about getting a new pony, but I was so upset I couldn't even think about it. In the end, Mom booked me on this vacation to try and cheer me up. That was only a couple of weeks ago, and she kept saying how lucky I was to get the last spot.

I tried to tell her that I didn't feel like riding, but she did that thing she does where she acts as if she's at work and bosses me around, saying things like, "Come on, darling, don't be silly about this, it'll be good for you."

Why can't she just see that I miss Apple so much it hurts? She wasn't just a pony to ride; she was my best friend!

I went down to wave to Mom, and when I got back upstairs, there was a girl sitting on the bottom bunk cuddling a really tattered toy rabbit. When I came in she stuffed it under her pillow, but I got Frieda the frog out of my suitcase, where I'd been hiding her.

The girl smiled and climbed up to sit on my bunk, bringing her rabbit with her. "Are you here on your own, too?" she asked.

She was relieved when I said that I was. She'd been worried that everyone would have friends here already.

Her name is Skye (and her rabbit is named

Sniff) and she's nine, like me. She's from Denver, which is kind of on the way back to my hometown from here. She has beautiful long, dark hair with some little braids and beads in it, and she's wearing a really cool pink tie-dye top. When I asked where she got it from, she said she'd dyed it herself! I'm going to try dying a couple of my T-shirts when I get home.

Then Olivia, Jess's daughter, came bursting in (turns out she's the owner of the messy bed by the window!). She climbed up on my bunk, too, and soon we were all chatting about what riding and stuff we'd done.

When Olivia told us she had her own pony, I ended

up admitting that I used to have one. I wasn't planning to tell anyone about Apple in case I got upset, but it just came out. Skye said she could imagine how I felt—her mom gave her cat away because of her baby brother being allergic to it. And Olivia said how she couldn't even bear to imagine selling her pony, Tally. I'm so relieved they don't think I'm spoiled for being upset when I've been lucky enough to have had my own pony in the first place. It's great knowing they understand.

Jess came up and sent us down to the yard just then. The other girls were there, and Sally and Lydia, and we had to go around in a circle and say our names and where we're from.

In the older girls' room there are:

Ricosha and Tanika are both 12 and they've come together from Carroll. Jordan is 11 and she's really giggly and silly, and she says she's always getting in trouble at school for talking during class!

The girls in the younger room are:

Yasmine is from Hillside, and Ruby and Molly have come together and live nearby. They're all eight.

Sally gave us these schedules so we can see roughly what we're doing each day, although she says it will change sometimes. In fact, it changed right away 'cos then we had a tour around the yard instead of a Pony Care lecture.

Pony Camp Schedule

8 a.m.: Wake up, get dressed, have breakfast
8:45 a.m.: Help in the yard, bring in the ponies from field, muck out stables, do feeds, etc.
9:30 a.m.: Prepare ponies for morning lessons (quick groom, tack up, etc.)
10 a.m.: Morning riding lesson
11 a.m.: Morning break—milk and cookies
11:20 a.m.: Pony Care lecture
12:30 p.m.: Lunch and free time
2 p.m.: Afternoon riding lesson
3 p.m.: Break—milk and cookies
3:20 p.m.: Pony Care lecture
4:30 p.m.: Jobs around the yard (i.e., cleaning tack, sweeping up, mixing evening feeds, turning out ponies)
5:30 p.m.: Free time before dinner
6 p.m.: Dinner (and cleaning up!)
7 p.m.: Evening activity
8:30 p.m.: Showers and hot chocolate
9:30 p.m.: Lights out and NO TALKING!

Sally showed us around Sunnyside and we all went WOW! when we saw the swimming pool and the game room. Then she took us into the main barn, where all the ponies who live outside in the summer were waiting for us. Lydia was busy tacking them up and getting them ready for our lesson and the other girls got really excited, wondering which ponies they were going to get and saying how cute they looked.

The barn smelled exactly like the one in my old yard, and without thinking I began looking for Apple among the ponies. With a start I realized what I was doing. That barn smell made me miss her so much! I was really relieved when we left to go to the fire drill meeting point.

Sally also went over some other safety things, like:

1. How to tie a pony up properly.

2. How important it is to put all the equipment away and not leave things lying around.

3. How you must always tell someone where you're going if you leave the group, even if it's just to go to the bathroom or to get a different grooming brush from the tack room.

4. The correct boots and hats and body protectors, of course!

Then we all had to practice tying slip knots in our lead ropes. Molly was having trouble, so I did hers, and then I did Ruby's, too, because she was looking a little bit confused. I'd tied up Apple so many times that I can do it with my eyes closed, so it was no big deal.

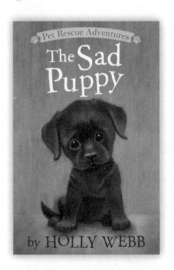

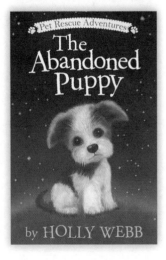

ANIMAL RESCUE CENTER

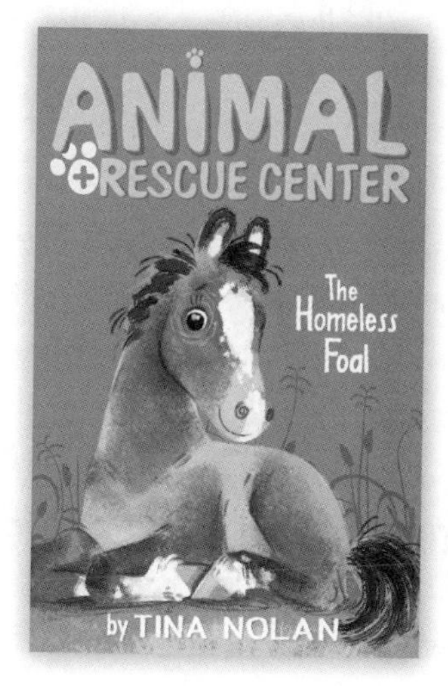

Kelly McKain

Kelly McKain is a best-selling children's and YA author with more than 40 books published in more than 20 languages. She lives in the beautiful Surrey Heath area of the UK with her family and loves horses, dancing, yoga, singing, walking, and being in nature. She came up with the idea for the Pony Camp Diaries while she was helping young riders at a summer camp, just like the one at Sunnyside Stables! She enjoys hanging out at the Holistic Horse and Pony Center, where she plays with and rides cute Smartie and practices her natural horsemanship skills with the Quantum Savvy group. Her dream is to do some bareback, bridleless jumping like New Zealand Free Riding ace Alycia Burton, but she has a ways to go yet!